ALBERT'S ALPHABET

by Leslie Tryon

ATHENEUM   1991   NEW YORK

COLLIER MACMILLAN CANADA
Toronto
MAXWELL MACMILLAN INTERNATIONAL PUBLISHING GROUP
New York   Oxford   Singapore   Sydney

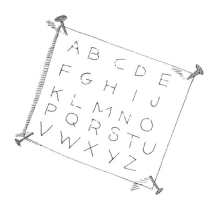

Special thanks to J, Eva, Con, Joy, Jo Ellen, Bev, and Gary

Atheneum
Macmillan Publishing Company
866 Third Avenue
New York, NY 10022

Collier Macmillan Canada, Inc.
1200 Eglinton Avenue East
Suite 200
Don Mills, Ontario M3C 3N1

First edition
Printed in the United States of America
1 2 3 4 5 6 7 8 9 10

Library of Congress Cataloging-in-Publication Data
Tryon, Leslie.
Albert's alphabet / written and illustrated by Leslie Tryon. —
1st ed.
p.   cm.
Summary: Clever Albert uses all the supplies in his workshop to
build an alphabet for the school playground.
ISBN 0-689-31642-9
[1. Alphabet. 2. Building—Fiction.] I. Title.
PZ7.T7865A1 1991
[E]—dc20

For my parents, Dorothy and Lester

Note to parents and teachers:

Part of the fun of *Albert's Alphabet* lies in the fact that Albert so carefully plans and uses every scrap of material he has before moving on to his more unusual creations. Children often love to pore over such details, allowing adult and child an opportunity to enjoy the book together again and again. It is also fun to note that all of Albert's building techniques—with perhaps a *little* bit of license here and there—follow common methods for cutting and joining in carpentry. As for his solution for the letter "Z"—well, he had to do it somehow!

Memo to:
Albert
School Carpenter

Good morning Albert,

Please build an alphabet for
the walking path on the
school playground. We must
have it by three o'clock this
afternoon.

If you have time will
you try to fix that leaky
old drinking fountain please?

Thank you
Principal
Pleasant Valley
School

Does Albert have enough time?

Does Albert have enough materials?

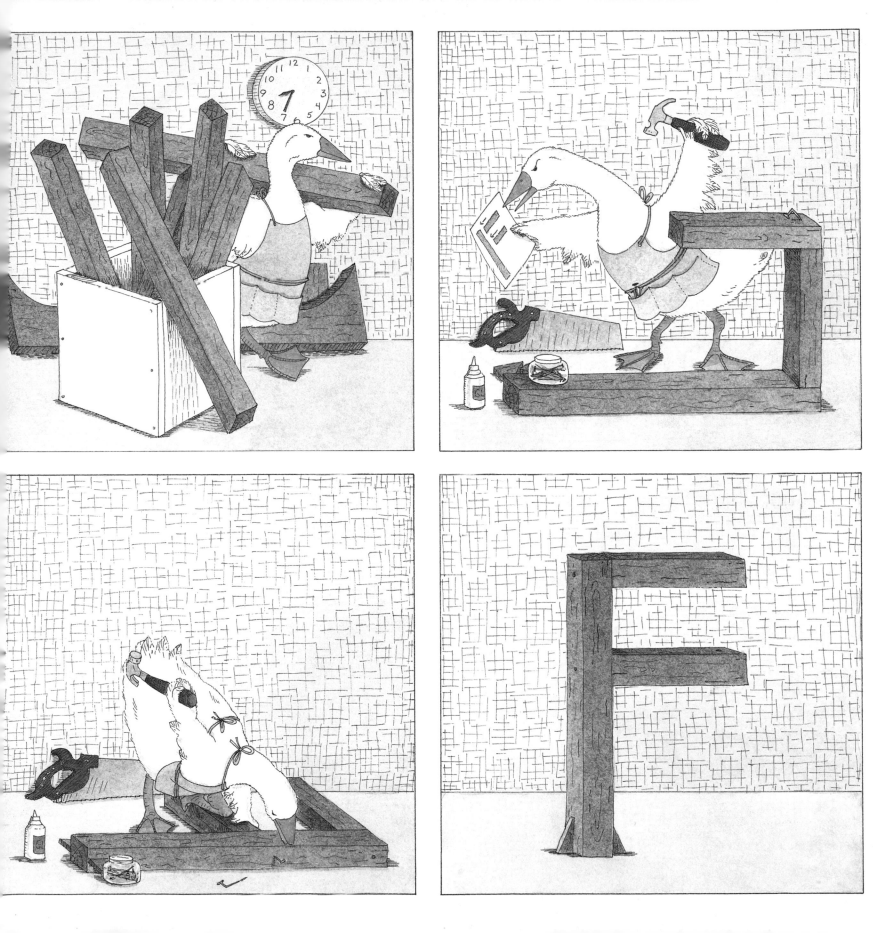

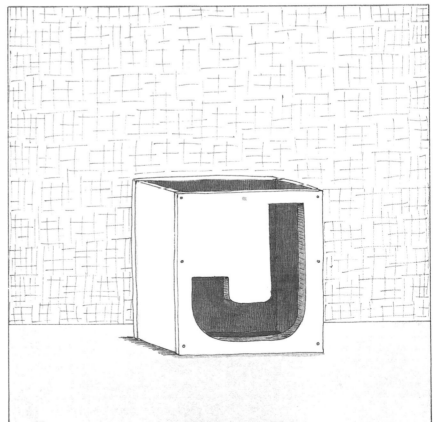

Oh Oh.
Albert used all of his lumber.
He used his box.

What will he use now?

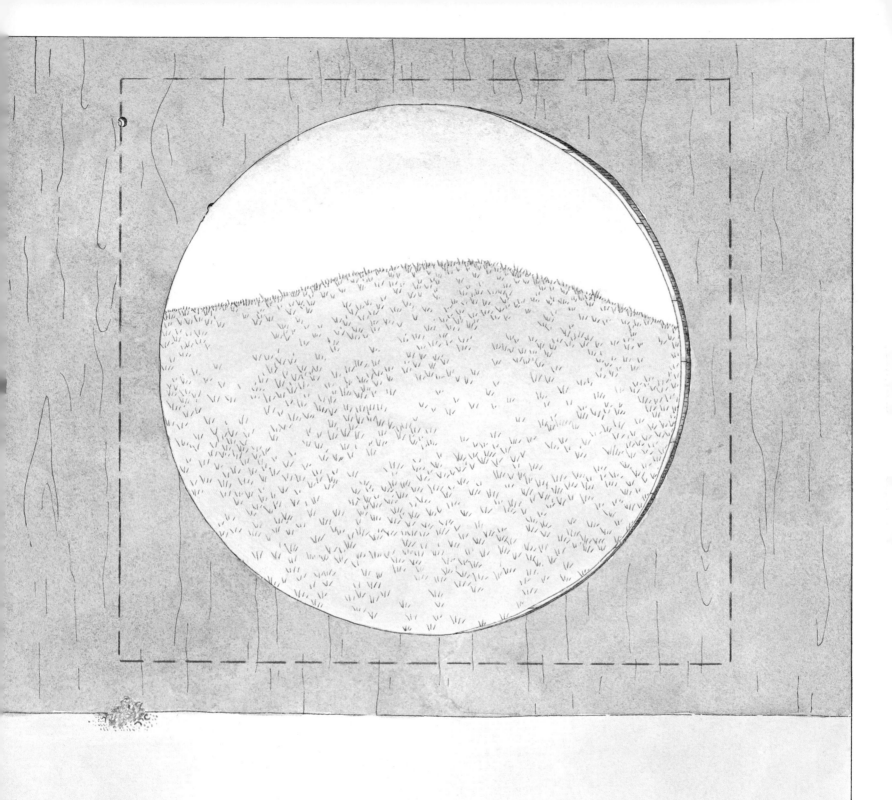

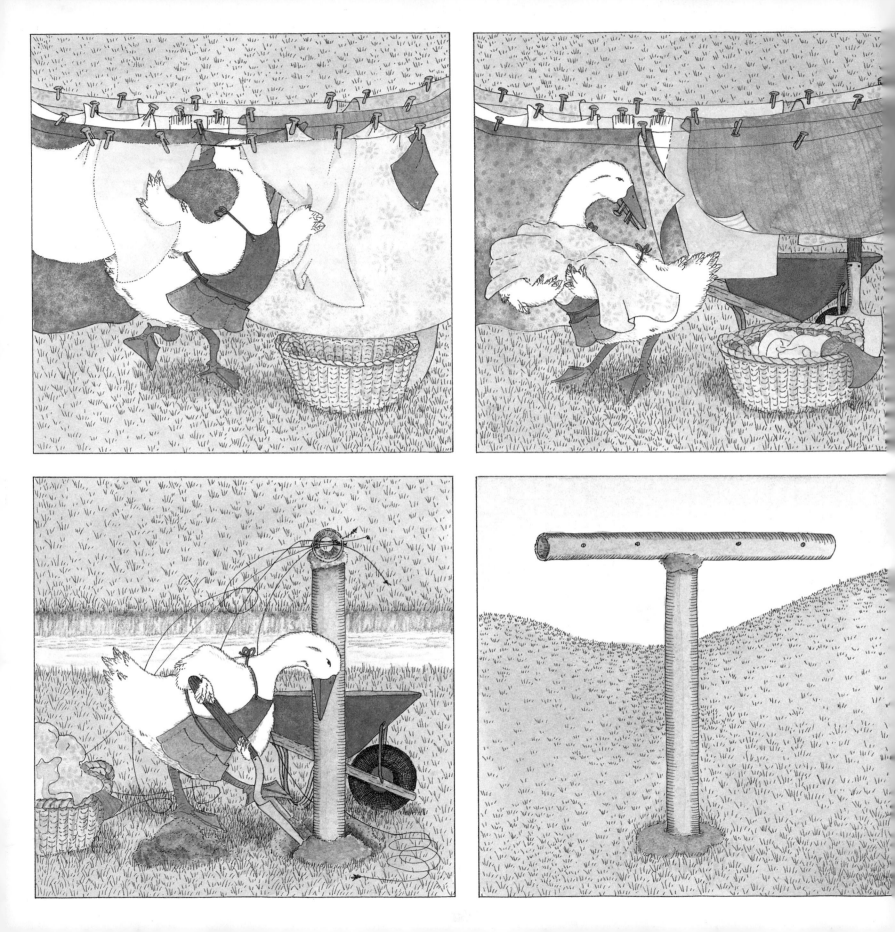

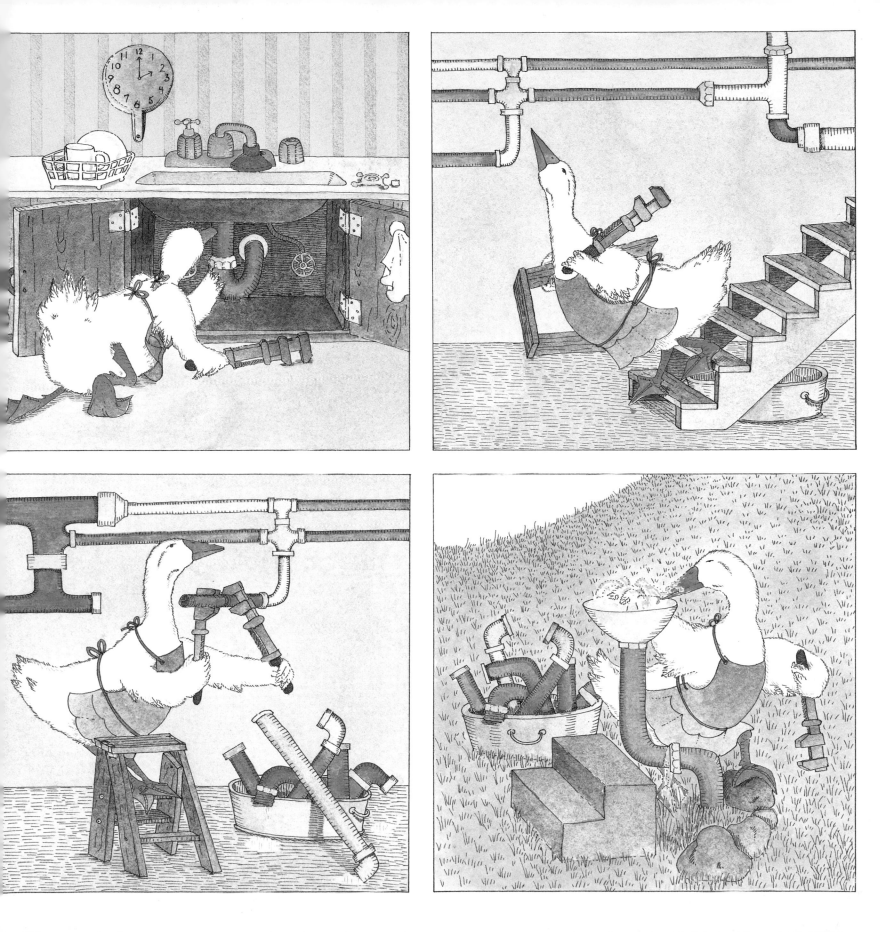

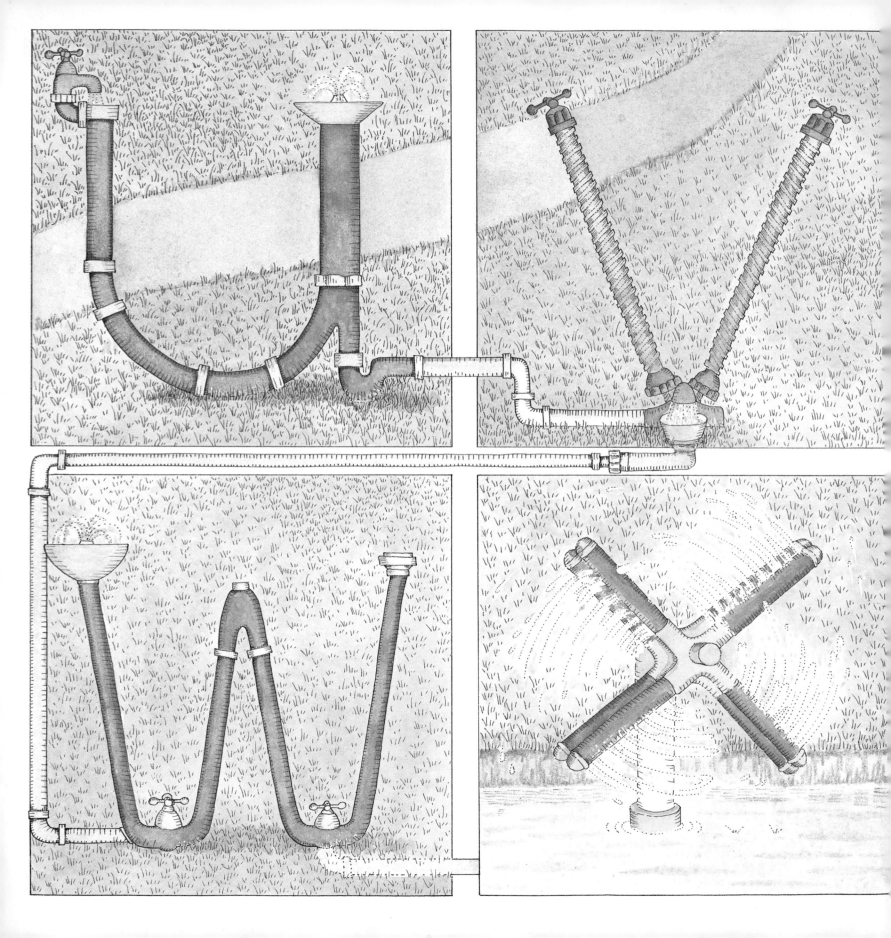

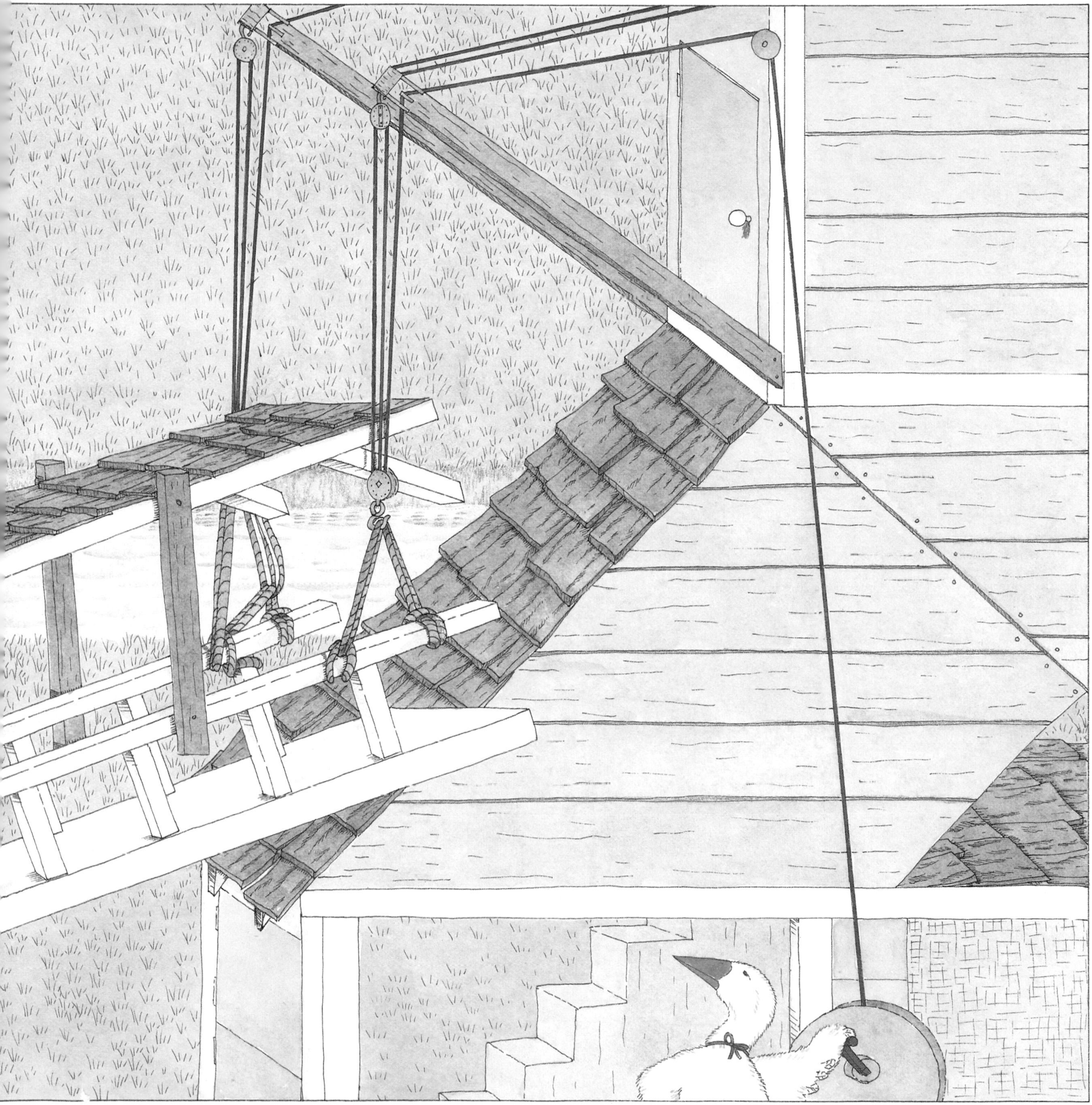

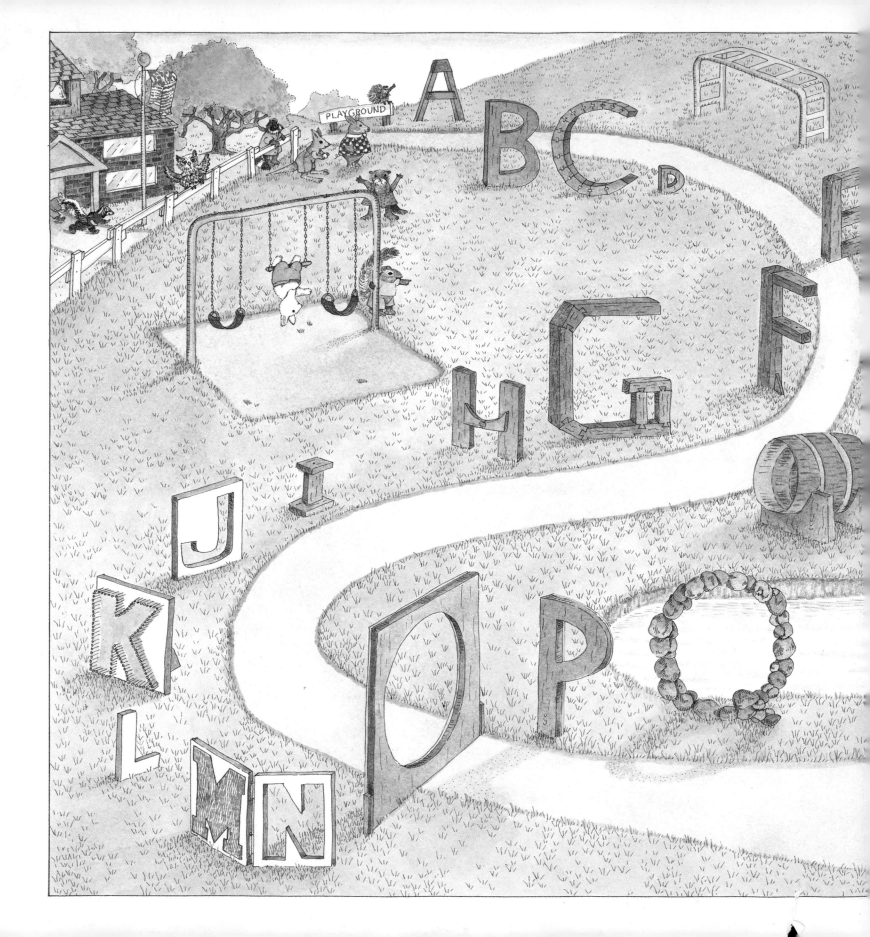